Merry Christmas, Strega Nona

STORY AND PICTURES BY
TOMIE de PAOLA

VOYAGER BOOKS
HARCOURT BRACE & COMPANY
San Diego   New York   London

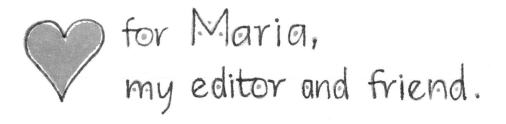
for Maria,
my editor and friend.

Library of Congress Cataloging-in-Publication Data
dePaola, Tomie.
Merry Christmas, Strega Nona.
Summary: Big Anthony plans a surprise Christmas
party for Strega Nona.
[1. Witches—Fiction. 2. Christmas—Fiction.]
I. Title.
PZ7.D439Me 1986   [E]   86-4639
ISBN 0-15-253184-X

K J I H

Printed in Mexico

The drawings were done in pencil, transparent colored inks, and watercolor on
140-lb. Fabriano handmade watercolor paper.
Color separations were made by Heinz Weber, Inc., Los Angeles, California.
Printed and bound by RR Donnelley & Sons Company, Reynosa, Mexico
Production supervision by Warren Wallerstein and Eileen McGlone
Typography design by G. B. D. Smith

It was the first Sunday of Advent,
and everyone in the little town in Calabria
was busy getting ready for Christmas.

Including Strega Nona — Grandma Witch.
She was busy getting everything ready
for the Christmas Eve feast
that she prepared every year.

Big Anthony, who worked for Strega Nona,
was being kept busy, too!

"Anthony," said Strega Nona, "don't dawdle!
There are only four weeks to *Natale* — Christmas —
and there is so much to do.
"The whole house must be cleaned,
and there is so much cooking and baking to do.
After all, everybody in the town will be here."

"Why can't Bambolona help?" whined Big Anthony.
Bambolona was the baker's daughter
who had come to stay with Strega Nona
and learn her magic.

"Bambolona has gone to help her father at the bakery, "
answered Strega Nona.

With Christmas coming, the poor baker was in such trouble
with so many people asking for special cakes and cookies
that he didn't even have time to sit in the square
with his friends.
Bambolona and Strega Nona felt sorry for him.
So Strega Nona sent Bambolona home to help.

"Why don't you help the baker out with your magic,
Strega Nona?" asked Big Anthony.
"No, not at Christmas!" said Strega Nona.
"Now, go shake out those feather beds."

"Anthony," said Strega Nona,
"run down the hill to the town and get me a new broom
so we can sweep the house from top to bottom."
"Oh, Strega Nona," said Big Anthony,
"can't we sweep the house with magic?"
"Not at Christmastime," said Strega Nona.
So Big Anthony went down the hill
to get a new broom.

Strega Nona worked hard
cleaning the house from top to bottom
as the days of Advent went by.

Each week she lit one more candle
on the Advent wreath.

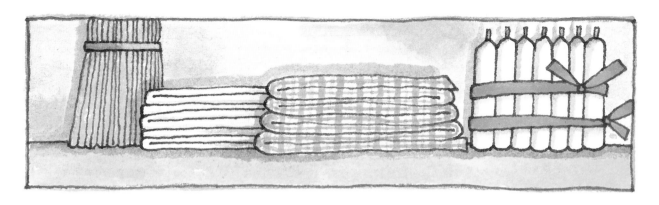

And each day, she sent Big Anthony
on an errand down to the town.
New brooms, new candles, new curtains,
new bedcovers, new tablecloth.
"Anthony," said Strega Nona,
"run down the hill and get me the *baccalà*—
the dried codfish for the Christmas stew.
And when you get back,
put it in the tub with water to soak it."
"Soak it?" asked Big Anthony.

"Yes," answered Strega Nona.
"Every day, until Christmas Eve, you must change the water
so the fish will be nice and soft
and not too salty for the Christmas stew."

"Can't your magic do all that?" asked Big Anthony.
"No, no magic at Christmastime," said Strega Nona.
"Christmas has a magic of its own."
So Big Anthony set off down the hill.

"Hello, Big Anthony," said one of the townspeople.
"How's Strega Nona?"
"Oh," said Big Anthony, "she's very busy
getting the house ready for Christmas.
Every day she sends me to town to get something.
Every day she has me helping her clean windows,
shake out the beds, paint the goat shed.
She's getting ready to cook all kinds of things.
I have to soak the codfish — the *baccalà* —
and change the water every day until Christmas Eve.
And I'm tired!"

"Don't you know
that Strega Nona loves *Natale*—Christmas?" a man from town asked.
"That's why she's so busy!
Why, she doesn't even have time to cure headaches
and make love potions and get rid of warts."
"Every year she cleans her house and prepares
a big feast and invites everyone," said a woman.
"She invites everyone?" asked Big Anthony.
"Everyone," said the woman. "Why, it wouldn't
seem *Natale* without the feast at Strega Nona's house."

"Hello, Big Anthony," said Bambolona,
who was on her way to the bakery.
"Are you in town
to buy Strega Nona a Christmas gift?"

"Oh, Bambolona,
I want to talk with you about that,"
said Big Anthony.

One by one the days went by,
and finally it was the day of Christmas Eve —
la Vigilia di Natale.

"Now, Anthony," said Strega Nona,
"here is a long list of things
for you to get for me—flour, eggs, butter, spices,
peppers, olives, oil, and sugar.
Hurry down the hill and hurry right home again,
for I have all kinds of things
to cook and bake."
"Oh, Strega Nona," Big Anthony complained,
"can't you use—?"
"NO MAGIC AT CHRISTMASTIME," said Strega Nona.
"Now go! I have to decorate the house
with the lemon blossoms and periwinkles."

Strega Nona waited and waited and waited.
No Big Anthony.
Finally the sun began to set,
and Big Anthony came whistling up the hill—
with empty hands.

"Anthony," said Strega Nona,
standing in the doorway of her little house,
"where have you been?"
"Oh, Strega Nona,
there was a Christmas puppet show in the town square.
It came all the way from Venice, up north."

"And where are all the things on my list?"
"Oh," said Big Anthony, "I forgot."

"Anthony, what am I going to do?
It's Christmas Eve.
There will be no cookies,
no *cenci* — fried pastry — no roasted peppers.
Oh, well, go get me the *baccalà*,
so I can at least make the fish stew."

Big Anthony came back
holding the codfish. It was as stiff as a board.
"I forgot this, too," said Big Anthony.
"I forgot to soak it in the water."
"Oh, Big Anthony, won't you *ever* learn!"
cried Strega Nona.

"Now it's too late to prepare anything
to eat for the feast."
"There's always your magic pasta pot,"
said Big Anthony timidly.
"No! I've told you before—NO MAGIC at Christmas,"
said Strega Nona.
"There will be no Christmas feast
at Strega Nona's this year!"

Strega Nona sent Big Anthony
to tell everyone not to come to her house for the feast.

She looked at the lemon blossoms and periwinkles
decorating the house.

Outside, she heard the *Zampognari*,
the shepherds from Abruzzi
who came all the way down to Calabria
to sing Christmas songs.

The bells rang.
It was time for the Midnight Mass.

Sadly,
Strega Nona went down the hill
to the church.
A fine Christmas this would be
with no company, no feast.

The townspeople whispered
as she went into the church.
"No feast," said one.
"Poor us," said another.
POOR Strega Nona.

When the mass was ended,
Strega Nona went up to the big manger scene
in the church.
There beside the Virgin and Saint Joseph
lay the Holy Child.

"Ah, *Bambino*," said Strega Nona,
"the night you were born
it was not like this manger scene,
with all these people.
You were all alone with your mama and Saint Joseph—
all alone, just like Strega Nona is tonight.
Ah—anyway—happy birthday, *Bambino*,
and *Buon Natale*."

And Strega Nona slowly left the dark church

and climbed the hill to her little house.

She opened the door—
and the room burst into light.
"Buon Natale—Merry Christmas, Strega Nona!"
everyone cried.
"This year, we're giving *you* a feast."
"Look," said Bambolona,
"codfish stew, roasted peppers,
cookies, and fried pastry."

"Oh, Bambolona," said Strega Nona,
"did you do all this for Strega Nona?"
"No, Strega Nona," said Bambolona.
"Big Anthony planned the whole surprise!"

"Bravo, Big Anthony!" everyone shouted.

"Merry Christmas, Strega Nona," said Big Anthony.

"Oh, Anthony, " said Strega Nona.

"You *have* learned! And with NO MAGIC."

"It's just like you said, Strega Nona."
Big Anthony smiled.
"Christmas has a magic of its own."